llama llama holiday drama

Anna Dewdney

SCHOLASTIC INC.

For the Luhrmann family

ISBN 978-0-545-27795-2

12   15 16 17/0

Printed in the U.S.A.   40

This edition first printing, November 2012

Set in ITC Quorum

Llama Llama holidays.
Jingle music. Lights ablaze.

HOLIDAY SALE

Sparkly candles. Yummy bread.
Dress-up clothes in green and red.

How long till that special date?

Llama Llama has to **wait.**

Llama Llama holidays.
Ads and signs and store displays.

ONLY 12 MORE
SHOPPING DAYS!

Fluffy snow and funny elves.
Goodies piled high on shelves.

Just **how many** days to go?
Llama Llama wants to know.

Time to buy and
search and shop.

Mama carries.   Llama drops.

Buy a friend a rubber duck?
Pirate ship or tractor truck?
Wooden blocks or
building set?

HOLIDAY SALE!

What will Llama Llama get?

Llama Llama holidays.
Hustle bustle.
Cooking craze.
Measure sugar.
Roll the dough.
Ten more batches
left to go. . . .

How many more days, again?
The special day
is coming **when?**

Take the cookies out to cool.
Frost a great big batch for school!

Add some sprinkles. Almost done. . . .
Teacher gets the fancy one.

No more cookies left to bake!

Llama Llama tummy-ache.

School has dreidels, songs, and bells.
Big red ribbons, woodsy smells.

Draw a snowman. Make a star.
Decorate a candle jar.

Are there many days to go? Llama time is going **slow....**

Mama needs a present, too!
Get some sparkles, sticks, and glue.

Roll it up and wrap it how?
Llama wants to give it **now!**

Llama Llama holidays.
Unpack stockings.
Unwrap trays.

Shiny silver.
Fancy plates.

Llama Llama
waits, waits, **waits.**

Cut out snowflakes.
Tape them up.
Pour some eggnog in a cup.

Oops! It's yucky on
the floor.

Llama Llama waits
some more.

Stringing lights is not much fun.
How come Mama isn't done?
Is the big day coming soon?
Llama Llama starts to **swoon**....

All this waiting for **one day?**

Time for presents **RIGHT AWAY!**

Too much music, too much fluff!
Too much making, too much stuff!

Too much **everything** for Llama . . .

Llama Llama, HOLIDRAMA!

Come and listen, little Llama.
Have a cuddle with your mama.

Sometimes we should take a rest
and hold the ones we love the best.

Wishing, waiting, wanting things . . .
we forget what this time brings.

Gifts are nice,
but there's another—
the true gift is
we have each other.

Llama Llama, warm and snug,
gives a kiss and gets a hug,
snuggles close with Mama Llama. . . .

Happy holidays for Llama.